THE RESCUED CHRISTMAS

WINGS - BOOK ONE

SMRITI

I have to say, that I dedicate this book - that is my first novel, to my beloved sister and my sweet mother! Their love and motivation always initiated the flight of my imagination.

Love you always, my two Angels! xoxo

- Smriti

Contents

Christmas is here, but so is the dark...

Violetta

10th December, The Present.

It was pitch dark and not a rumble was heard when suddenly, down the orange lighted streets of a ghastly alley, sound of brisk steps was heard heading towards some unknown destination. Someone was walking in silence but didn't seem to have very generous motives. "Clamp!" The figure opened and shut the door of some old vendor's hut, at its back. As for now, there was a burning fireplace in the hall, the figure was quite visible. It was a woman, but something was more to her. She practically appeared to be a Witch! With those long ebony black locks, streaked with hints of deep violet, a thin and long hat and completely dressed in black. As if she was trying not to catch any attention. "Hmm... what's up with you? Are you ready yet, or not?" She said with the last words coming out as a scream almost. "Ooh, you better NOT speak in that tone! Or else I will --- anyways, I am here with a deal. If you want me to do as you wish, then I would like to have a nice pay for that, not just for me but for my whole clan! So, what do you offer miss?" There he sat, in a corner on a weak armchair with a curved corner of his lips; dressed in shabby clothes and a very short height though he had a long tongue. He had teeth like a monster and long dirty claws with bulging eyes! Well, yes, he was an Imp. A dark underworld creature known for its bloodlust and ruthlessness. "Oh! You Imps don't realize that you can't stand a chance against us Witches! But that's a topic for some other time. I have come here with important business. You will be paid generously...you just need to assure me that my work will be done!" As she said this, she took off her precious emerald studded necklace and threw it on his face. The Imp seemed to take in the smell of the gemstones and finally said, "worry not my lady, DOOM shall cover Fairyland!"

Magic Meadow

(ONE AND A HALF MONTHS BACK)

The sun shone brightly up above in the sky, hidden between the bright white clouds! A soft breeze blew by the roads surrounded with hills, carrying a sound of gentle chimes. Yes, you are right! It was the sweet town of Magic Meadow in the beautiful State of Fairytopia. Fairies lived happily in their lands without any worries but, if required, always prepared for a challenge! "Trickle-trickle" Beautiful clear crystalline waterfalls flowed from the hill tops and down they went to the bed of valleys full of green flora covered in slight layer of silver snow. The leaves had started fading their greens away and turning into brittle golden and auburn coloured instead! Yes! Autumn was here along with the onset of a heavy snowfall and tiny little birds sang songs of cry and joy in their nests. Deep down the valleys and at the foot of hills was a small yet flourishing town named as Magic Meadow. "Swoosh!" A cleanliness worker was brooming away the excess yellow and half yellow leaves as well as dirt from the footpaths of the main city road. "Hmm, what a fine day I wish I could get myself some cola", said the worker. "Well, here is your cola sir! Actually, I was having a spare one so I thought you should have it instead!" Shouted a young girl, flashing a bright smile at the worker with white teeth, short height, little chubby figure and dressed in a pink flowy skirt and a golden crop top! "Why, my name is Rose and you are --- " "Rose come on! You are so very kind and equally talkative my dear little friend!" shouted another shrill voice, full of feminine touch and admirable dominance at the same time. "Oh! Jasmine, you are so bossy! I would have rather gone alone!" "No no, I wouldn't have let you go alone! God-knows-who would be the next prey of your sweet little talks, wanting just something to EAT in return!" The two girls who were actually Besties, went walking down the road towards the city park, 'CRYSTAL COVEN'. Well, truly it was a magnificent place! There were green tendrils hanging on the gate and in the centre was a pleasant fountain which glimmered in several colours at night. Ah! to much of our surprise, there were some other youngsters about the same age waiting for these two. There was one girl, in black jeans and a hoody, surrounded by two young boys who were constantly pacing right and left. One of them was a bit worried, with furrowed brows, as if he had been waiting for someone special. The other one was strolling by the tree, with a book in his hands, he didn't seem to care for the rest of the world! He wore a dark blue jeans and a loose purple T-shirt with a denim overcoat. God-knew-what was going on this young fellow's mind. Soon, the gate screeched open and the two girls dashed in! Rose shouted in delight, "Hey Alice! We are back, and you know what--" " Ya ya, leave it all please. We are all here for a reason so let's not delay guys. Agreed?", Jasmine said with a tired voice. "Agreed!" Everyone screamed except that loner boy lost in his book. "Ahem?"

Jasmine coughed, "are you there Terence Williams?" "Oh, well, do I look like I am somewhere else Jasmine Willows?" "You--" "Let's get to the point, tomorrow is a very big function in our academy in regards to Christmas. So, we need to discuss our preparations neatly in an organized way." Rose grunted, " well, I would prefer a sweet warm arrangement! What do you say Brandon, Alice?" "Uhh, I think, you, better stay with me as you cause trouble", said Brandon while taking hold of Rose's arm in a swift movement. Alice immediately rolled her eyes and Jasmine started feeling awkward while her cheeks went pink, " Okay, so we will be planning a warm and bold get together in the school tomorrow" said Jasmine shyly, though struggling to hide her shyness! After a long time spent with gossiping about decorations and munching on snacks, they said goodbye to each other and....the night set in. All the friends went to bed for a sweet slumber. The moon started fading away with light of rising sun and in a few hours, morning was here. "Beep-beep", oh! What a useless alarm it was! Poor Jasmine couldn't help but punch it! "What the actual---forget it! It's time Jasmine, get ready for school, come on be quick! Uhh, ok so what will I wear today? I guess it should be something elegant and fancy as it's a BIG DAY today! So, well, what have we got.... hmmm," as she was searching her little wooden, polished wardrobe frantically, a beautiful light teal dress with a delicate lavender lace on the neck cut and on the cuffs; caught her eye. It was gifted by her maternal grandmother on her last birthday which all five of them had celebrated in a small cottage near the sea shore! Well, yes... here 'five of them' definitely means that she had siblings. Yes, she had two brothers, one was thirteen-year-old and the youngest was eight years old, their names were Linden and Timmy. It can be said that

Jasmine had a nice cozy family, if you ignore the way her two nasty little brothers smashed a whole double decker cake on her face, as a birthday gift, every year! Anyhow, she considered herself lucky to have a cute little loving family. "I think it's ok, umm, no it's good, really good! I just need a sober hairstyle, which would be, ah! This!" And she took a shimmering rubber band as she tied her lovely chocolate brown hair in a high pony. She swirled in front of the mirror and was picking her bag when she heard a loud horn, blowing... "beep--beep". The bus! It was on the door! "Oh no, not late again!" she thought in panic. After all, *'old habits die hard.'*

II

In the flash of a moment, she ran to the door and headed straight for the bus. She couldn't miss this day at her school, not only because it was a big day regarding Christmas Eve but also that she was the girls' monitor in the class and she was bound to some responsibilities! "You will never learn Jasmine, leave it, let's go!", said the conductor and up they went! Now, 'up' here means LITERALLY up! Wow! What a scene it was, clouds everywhere! Yes, they were flying in the sky! Vast blue expanse everywhere, with white and silver floating clouds, the whole Magic Meadow was visible from that view. Fairies usually had pleasures like this often, "umm, my cupcake looks just like clouds! right Jasmine?", Rose shrieked in delight when she felt a little slap on her head. "You fool, the frosting looks like the cloud, not the cupcake!" said Jasmine. "Oh, so we are discussing cupcakes, aren't we?", echoed a deep voice from behind the girls' heads, it was Brandon. He was quite fond of his friend Rose specially, while he pretended to be the exact opposite! As these three were chatting, two more joined them, Alice and 'Mr. Weirdo', Terence. After some time, the bus landed on a soft muddy ground on which the Cloud Castle Academy stood, as we know it was up in the sky but even there it needed a base so, yes there it stood, its top towers reaching the highest clouds, it was like a floating island in the middle of the vast blue sky! Terence had already got down from the bus and was headed towards the main gate when suddenly Jasmine caught up with him, running literally, breathing heavily. "Hey! I need to talk to you", she said. He turned and stared right at her face with such a fierce expression that she literally felt the urge to flee, but it was important. So, she stammered a little and then said, "I-I need to tell you that, I had to return your history note book, thanks for the notes, Terence." Without a word he took his note book and turned on his heels, as if trying to hide something? Well, whatever it was Jasmine had no idea about it and she was a carefree fairy you know, she was thinking all this when Rose took her by her arm and off, they went to their class... Standard 'IX Ruby.'

Well, it was quite a scene you know, as every student in the class was either busy throwing white paper balls at each other or touching up their final makeup, not the boys of course! "Hush! keep quiet! Miss Sofia will soon be coming down the corridor and I certainly don't want to ruin my reputation as the girls' monitor!" shouted Jasmine, nearly forcing the air out of her lungs. There were almost thirty students in their class which included some hippie boys and judgmental girls, never mind that! Not a pleasant news but yes, there were some girls 'jealous' of the 'Mystery Gang', not only because they used to be the most mysterious & appreciated students, but also because these girls thought that Jasmine and Rose were quite lucky to be around the school's most handsome boys. Not to mention Alice, as people wondered, "was she really a girl?" A question for another time. So, it was clear that these five were the odd ones out definitely, however, they had something in common within their group, that they loved adventures, mysteries and magic! This was true as all five of them were really focused and dedicated in regards with their chosen subjects in studies. Yes, Cloud Castle was a Fairy school, so, there was no burden of studying 'everything'. You could easily choose your subjects according to your magical abilities. Thus, 'Give freedom and take inspiration' was the greatest 'motto' of this academy. (Not to miss, a little bit of Fairy Dust, could always sparkle up your lives!) Jasmine was always inclined towards Nature and the simple beauty of life and thus dreamt of taking Nature Magic as her main subject with some other side subjects when she would pass XII standard, whereas Rose, was a true 'fairy princess' as she decided to pursue, Royalty Magic & Beauty studies as her field and dreamt of becoming a Lady Royal in the Fairy Queen's Court! In the same way, Alice was passionate about boxing and sports, so she chose to be a little non-magical fairy, but true, she had her own inherited magical powers of gemstones and healing. And then came 'the boys', Brandon was a tall & lean fairy with dark chestnut hair and a knack for mixing things up! Actually, in simpler words, Potions & enchanted brews! On the other hand, Terence was a typical 'Techno' you know, so he would go with Technical Magic which also included Psychic Magic and Mind Reading. *That,* was quite definitely, one of the reasons why people stayed away from him, other than his intimidatingly masculine appearance, however, he was lean and tall as well with dark brown hair and fierce hazel eyes burning with some vague feeling.... God knew what. "So, that's what this class is about today huh?" He asked with a mocking gesture, to Jasmine. Before she opened her mouth to reply, the door to the class opened with a 'thud' and there she was, Miss Sofia, their class in charge. "So ready for some lessons, are we?" She said, with a slight twist of her mouth.

That period really did go bad, full-time lectures and scoldings, but nonetheless, after it was over, the students finally relaxed. Only getting ready for a bigger announcement in the next one. "Shh! Can't you see the principal is coming down that last corridor!" Rose let out a silent scream. "Well, I guess this business right there in the main hall is really important Rose. It's better if we hurry now" Jasmine remarked and all five of them along with their line went down the corridor, straight to the main hall of Cloud Castle. It was quite a huge hall and now, for some unknown reason, it was completely decorated with glittering gold and silver balloons and little shimmering light sparks suspended in the air! It really was breathtaking. As the students were settling down in their comfy leather chairs, the head boy and the head girl of Cloud Castle stepped forward. They made their welcome speech when, the principal did the honours. "I guess by now you all must be curious, as for what is this gathering for? Hmm...I think my fellow students of The Cloud Castle are going to face three other very famous academies! These academies will be represented by hundred students from each one of them. They are here, as for their little excursion trip and now, welcome the first academy, 'The Genietopia Academy!'" There was a huge round of applause for the Genies appearing on the stage one by one, out of the blue. They were translucent in appearance and dressed in traditional outfits with tons of gold ornaments! The boys were wearing *salwar* and a small over coat on their bare chests and the girls were dressed in either *salwar* or Arabic style gowns. These were no ordinary dresses, just as they looked from their exterior. They were special silk from the Western countries. "Whooo!", there went a loud hooting by the boys, as usual. Then came the Elves from 'The Academy of Hexis', all quite tall than normally expected and clothed in formal outfits such as tight pants and shirts for boys and skirts and crop tops for girls. Not to forget their 'unique mark', their long narrow ears! One could say that the elvish girls were really pretty! Most of them had long & dark beige or golden hair with pink cheeks and thin frame. "Wow! These Elves and Genies, as well, are so mesmerizing!" said Rose with a suppressed squeak. "Well, I think someone is even prettier, isn't it?" asked Brandon with little smile tugging at the corner of his mouth. "Who?" She simply didn't get the hint and was about to enquire further when a voice broke the temporary silence, "So, students let's welcome our last guests, the Witches from Witchtopia's, Wiggenweld Academy!" 'Swoosh!' There went a broom over the head of one of the fairies, and then other and another! There were brooms in the air with powerful and bold witches on top of them!

III

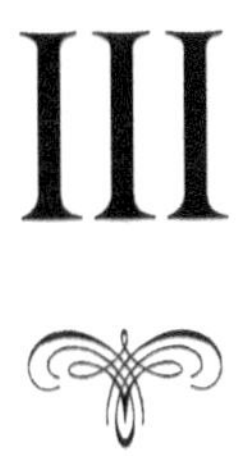

There was a wave of excited & loud cheers among the witches as they cleared the way for their principal's daughter, the princess of Wiggenweld Academy, Violetta. She was slim and trim whereas her two 'bodyguard' friends, on her either side, were little chubby. Violetta wore a stunning magenta gown with black frills and she had long ebony black hair with streaks of violet. "This is Percy, my best friend", she said with a tired gesture, as if tired of introducing her friend. "Oh, hi to you Percy and you too, Violetta" Jasmine said proudly as if she was the head girl. Scratch that. "I am Jasmine Willows and these are my friends Brandon, Rose, Alice and uhm, Terence." Except for him, everyone else stepped forward but he stood there with a book in his left hand and a naive expression. "Hi" he said. "Uhh, hey guys what about some mocktails?" asked Brandon with an effort to lighten the mood. Well, the mood did lighten as, Violetta and her friends accepted the offer and were brought up to the cafeteria. Yummy, what an aroma it was! The smell of crushed coffee beans, hot chocolate, freshly baked cookies, sweet cheese-cakes & pastries... was spread in the air! One could admit that their school's cafeteria was way too good to be true. There were hanging paintings on the walls, depicting ancient fairy history. They were really awe inspiring to look at! And then there was a main order counter where a young, humble and stout man stood with a thick bunch of sheets in one hand and an ink pen in the other. Obviously, he was writing down the orders, when Violetta approached him and gave an order of almost three sheets! "Wow! What was that?" asked Rose with genuine curiosity. "Can't you see? We are three friends, so one sheet's order, for one." This...was a bit shocking truly! How could these witches eat so much and still have a slim body? Never mind, Rose could think about that later, of course. Time flew by, and it was just about to be dusk when the school bell rang and the children returned to their buses respectively; when a flock of birds emerged in the sky somewhat coming from the school's direction. "Hmm, I guess this winter many more migratory birds will be seen in the town" Alice remarked. But as the flock came closer it appeared as magical flyers instead of birds! 'Swishh!' The flock of flyers collided with the buses and started falling into the windows! Someone picked one up and read it out loud,

'Dear fellow students and teachers,

we are pleased to inform you that our Magical Academy, Cloud Castle will be hosting three consecutive gatherings in honour of our special guests. These parties will be theme based according to each & every single Academy and will be starting from tomorrow! So, enjoy yourselves while you maintain the discipline.

Love and regards,

Principal Isabelle.

"Soo that's a news right!? We are going to party! What do you think Jasmine, what would be the themes and the dress codes?" "Oh, please Rose, don't start again. All I am thinking about is that I really hope these Wiggenweld Witches don't create a scene you know!" That was the last line that she could speak, as the bus roared with its engine starting and they were off to their 'down town' homes! That evening the one who suffered the most was none but Terence. Why? Because his little sister, ok, his little wicked sister, Lily had eaten all his chocolates and spilled hot coffee on his history notes! Hah! Such a poor thing. The next morning, all the five friends were dressed in their most fancy yet traditional outfits as, it was the day to honour the Genies! Rose was dressed in a silver *salwar* with a white sleeveless top and a high pony whereas Alice was wearing a tight black *kurta* with a black long skirt along with a fishtail. Her hair was quite peculiar as it was dark gold colour with pinch of natural, biscuit shade highlights. Rose was chatting with Alice when suddenly her heart skipped a beat for no reason! The sight that made this happen was actually, Brandon walking towards the bus stop, tall and lean, with his school bag on his back. He was wearing a Dark Peach coloured *salwar* and a silver overcoat with a thin *kurta* under it. Rose didn't quite understand why her heart was beating so fast, but never mind, she hugged him lightly and he held her with a unique warmth. It was the second they broke apart when, a sound of someone colliding, came banging in their ears! Oh, it was nothing much but just that Terence and Jasmine had collided into each other and now she was very awkwardly hanging in his strong arms just above the ground. "What the hell!? Leave me!" she screamed in rage when he suddenly dropped her to the ground and walked ahead as if nothing had happened! At that exact moment the bus came and everyone hurried inside out of some weird embarrassment. Finally, it was the time for the party to begin after they had their brunch in the cafeteria. "Oof!

What a look!" a girl pointed out to Terence as she passed by their group, standing in the corner of the main hall. Truly Terence was a sight for your eyes! His black *salwar* and golden *kurta* were standing out! But wait, Jasmine was no less. She literally looked like a Genie Goddess! She wore a beige gown with gold jewellery and her hair was tied in a low bun with little pearls on her head. Their little chit chat couldn't last long as the music was put on and the people went crazy! A huge meal was organized for everyone, and it was a real good party. Just the same way the gathering for the sweet and notorious Elves was also arranged the other day, where everyone wore long bell-shaped outfits and jingled boots with stylish pants. That night, it was so tiring for all five of them that they fell asleep early, after finishing their dinner.

After a few hours, the Sun came up over the horizon and dawn set in. "Jasmine! wake up! breakfast is ready!" her mother, Carol Willows shouted with her full power. It was fifteen minutes past eight and the bus was going to arrive in just twenty minutes! "Woah! Why are you such a sleepy head Jasmine?!" she murmured to herself, ignoring her mom's scoldings, and headed straight for the bathroom. Then she dressed herself up in a witchy costume and rushed downstairs with her bag. 'Oh! I am so sorry Mom, here I am. What is the breakfast--" 'beep-beep!' Oh no! It was the bus. Jasmine calmed herself down, picked up a honey pancake and dashed towards the stop. Thankfully, she didn't miss it and she sat down next to Rose who was dressed as a Flower Witch! Alice, well, as always was a little tomboy-ish and wore jeans and a crop top with skeleton print. Terence and Brandon were both sitting at the back and were dressed as impressive dark warlocks! Yes, it was the last day of welcome gatherings and it was the day to honour the witches. Those witches who had insulted the fairies! But the fairies were not the same. They believed in affection and sincere good will. So, as they reached the main hall, which was this time decorated with dark green smoke and almost no lighting, they collided with who else, but Violetta! "Oh! I see that you fairies can't even watch your steps!" She admonished them, disgustingly. "Sorry" said Rose softly, clearly not rising to the bait. But immediately a hand intercepted her. "Why are you saying sorry? It's not our fault" said Brandon with a grunt. "It's ok Brandon, hush." "But--" "Okay, okay! Stop it guys. We are all big enough to control ourselves, right? So, Violetta sorry we made you stop in your tracks but you could also have kept your eyes on your steps" Jasmine said with a mocking gesture towards her feet. At this Violetta's huge ego was hit, "You will pay for messing with me you---" and at that exact moment Terence came forward and shielded Jasmine with his body. "Don't. You. Dare. Speak. A. Word." He said, his hazel eyes flaring with anger. Gosh! The scene was really heating up, and exactly when the DJ put a disco song on those speakers! Everyone was rising to the bass' beats whereas, the 'Fabulous Five' were all pissed off. Violetta stroked a lock of her hair, pushing it back on her shoulder and then strode forward with a cold & unaffected expression. One could only hope that, no more scene would be created and this day would have a 'Happy Ending' too.

IV

"**Y**ou didn't need to do that. I could have handled myself" said Jasmine slowly but with an unrealistic & forced ego. "Oh, did you really think I did that, for you? I shooed her off because she was wasting our time!". This time Terence was really infuriated. How was this possible that Terence Williams would do something for someone *and* specially for his biggest competition?! Was it? No. Certainly not. One could rather solve this mystery later! But the point of competition was a little serious. Actually, for Terence it was pretty provoking, as he always got second position in the class because Jasmine secured the first position almost every time! And THAT hit his male ego like anything! This was one of the biggest reasons, why these two didn't fit together. Although they used to be really good buddies when they were quite young, like six or seven years old. Hmm, sad, but life goes on, one doesn't know what life has in exchange of one loss! It might be another beautiful gift, could it be? Maybe but that's a discussion for some other time. "Okay guys, now can we enjoy the party?" asked Alice with a tired face. It really was tiring to stand in a corner and chat about some petty thing, when the whole school was enjoying the Witches' Witchy, decor party with spooky little pumpkin lamps on the entrance, the huge size chandelier hanging in the middle of the main hall studded with pure green emerald stones and green flame candles! Wow! What a vision it was! Surely these witches must be filled with pride and a feeling of 'coming home again!' It was really lavish; the stage was covered with green climbers and witch hazels were hanging as flowers on the ceiling. There was a big cauldron in the middle of the sitting area, from which little charming gifts were popping out at an interval of ten seconds, whenever someone would come near it the clear water of the cauldron would change its colour according to the person's wishes! Sometimes it would be red, if the wish is very strong and passionate and sometimes yellow or light pink, if the person is calm and relaxed! The Fairies, Elves, Genies and Witches were all standing in groups and chatting with echoing sounds of merry laughter as well as some were dancing on the main stage, showing off their talents and moves. Similarly, these five friends were also standing near the cauldron and gossiping over soft drinks or mocktails... uhm, the latter were the girls only! Not boys of course! They both were sipping their drinks silently and watching the party with an exchange of a few sentences. That was exactly when something caught Jasmine's eye, an elf was approaching Violetta with a mug of coffee in his hands and was looking quite nervous. "What is he up to?" she thought. Then she heard the sounds of cheer and wicked laughter as she realized what was going on! They had definitely bet on Violetta and that Elf must have lost! So now, he was going to spill that coffee on her! Oh no! "Shit! Rose, please hold my glass for a second? I will be back." "But wait -- what? --- Jasmine!" And she dashed forward to save Violetta and everyone else from her rage when by mistake her right heel slipped on the polished floor and her left hand caught the mug of coffee, preventing it from spilling but she herself fell on Violetta and they hit the edge of the table next to them! "Ooh! I am so sorry Violetta! Are you okay?" said Jasmine trying to get up in a respectful way, while she offered a hand to her companion in this terrible fall. But the reality hit her hard! Violetta got up in one swift motion and snapped! However, her eyes were fixed on something else than the girl who fell on her, Jasmine. "What are you looking at---are you ok? --" "WHAT THE HECK! You broke my mother's last gift for me! You broke my mother's ring!! I WILL KILL YOU! ---" Just at that moment the boys stepped in, and shielded Jasmine! For the first time, Terence spoke with a little pity in his voice as well as terror, "Violetta you need to understand that she did not intend to hurt you. She was rather saving you from a filthy prank and---" "JUST SHUT UP!! All of you will pay the price for this day! For this insult!" she spoke in pure anger and dashed towards the cauldron. "What is she doing?!" Asked Rose in a scared voice when the suspense was broken. The second she peeped into the cauldron; the colour of the water turned Black! Slow ripples were forming in its centre and something evil could have been granted easily... when suddenly, the lid of the cauldron flew back on its top and a shrill voice shouted, from the entrance door. It was Principal Isabelle! "What is going on here? What is up with you Violetta? Don't even think of doing one of your dark spells in our territory!" "Hahaha! Your Territory? Well, maybe yes, but soon it won't be yours anymore! I will show you fairies, that you have nothing to be proud of! I will make sure of that! Now, Wiggenweld witches, follow me! We are leaving this moment, and will return soon with a proper revenge! Goodbye Fairies", she said with a wicked smile and off they went on their brooms, into the dark, night sky!

This couldn't be any worse. The Wiggenweld witches were now against fairies. Wow. God knows what revenge they must be planning against them! The mystery gang had gone back to their homes and everyone was silent. Maybe they just didn't know what to speak or share with their family members, so all of them slept quietly as night descended wholly. This was exactly how days passed by, mornings came and then night set in. Not a single fairy had thought that there would be such a time when the smiles would hide fear and worries, like a well-worn mask.... But so, did the Fate.

10th December, The Present, Magic Meadow

At present, everything was completely normal in the city of Magic Meadow. But so wasn't the case elsewhere. We already know about that! For the people of Fairyland, who were entirely unaware of the looming threat, it was like a thunderstorm cloud had just passed. But who could have imagined that it was quiet only to burst one day!? It was twenty minutes past three of midnight, when Jasmine suddenly felt something outside her bedroom window. She woke up immediately as her fairy powers never failed her. "Hmm, that must be the leaves rustling, it's ok, sleep Jasmine" she told herself and was ready to dream again when, a weird looking owl appeared on the branch of the apple tree that was close to her window! The weirdest part was that its eyes were bloodshot red! "Hoot--hoot!" It started hooting wildly as if getting impatient. Jasmine immediately calmed down her senses and quietly approached the window which was half open. "What do you want? What type of owl are you? I have never seen you here, before." She murmured to the bird, slowly. The owl turned around and lifted its left wing only to reveal a hidden parchment of old paper. She took the paper in her hands and the mysterious owl, flew away; as if it was only waiting to deliver some secret message! Jasmine was in utter confusion when she decided to open the letter and sat down on her bed to read it quietly,

"Some peace before the storm? Just wait and watch, fairy." That's it! That was all, that was written on that paper. But to her surprise it smelled a little strange. It almost was stinking! But a different kind of smell, something thick, metallic and irony. Yes, it was written in blood. By God's grace she suppressed a shriek as this realization hit her and her hand immediately went to her mouth. Otherwise, she would have woken everyone up and then it would have caused a great scene! Never mind, the terror had started. The dark had set its foot in Magic Meadow and could be a dangerous threat to the entire Fairyland! "Who could have done this? Oh my god! Is it Violetta? No, no! It can't be! I have to tell this to someone, at least my friends. I must sleep now so that I can wake up early tomorrow and call a group meeting in the 'Crystal Coven' ", she resolved. But the saddest part was that she simply couldn't sleep all night and exhausted her brain by thinking of & fearing the worst. Hours passed, and the first rays of morning Sun touched her eyelids gently, as if trying to tell that do not worry, good will always win! But one could still not know, what the future had in store for them.

It was ten minutes past eleven, when Jasmine's not so deep sleep broke off by a shrill sound. Actually, it was her phone ringing! 'Tring-tring!' That was really disturbing, after being woken up with a huge tension on the mind. Well, no matter what, she had to pick it up. And who was it? It was a group call from their little chatting group 'Fabulous Five'. Which would mean, something big had happened! She answered finally, "Oh! I am so sorry friends; I was sleeping and---" "Oh please! Now stop giving excuses Jasmine! We all know that Terence texted something last night in the group and still, you didn't come to the meeting?!" shouted Alice, nearly breaking the microphone! Oh my god! How could she miss it? How had Jasmine been so careless? That's exactly what she was thinking right at that moment. "But, I-I didn't know---" that's it, the call was cut! Wow, amazing. Now even her friends were not by her side! But wait, what had actually happened that the meeting was so urgent?? The thought raced in her mind and she quickly dressed up and ran downstairs. "Mom, I will have to leave for a while because of some important issue. Okay? Bye!" she said and hurried down her mansion's front pathway, which was incredibly beautiful! Definitely, it was not the most perfect time to admire its beauty but she couldn't help but glance at the hanging blue bells from tall trees and the little fairy lights decorated on the branches, which were still shimmering. At last, she reached her main gate and literally ran across the road straight towards, Crystal Coven! There they were! Sitting under a peach tree and discussing something very seriously. Just as they saw Jasmine coming, they stood up and put on stern expressions. "Hi, Jasmine. Very punctual right?" Rose said before rolling her 'burnt sienna' coloured eyes. "Hey, I know it's bad but at least you guys can hear me out?". Terence immediately waved his left hand in the air and clearly rejected her humble offer! "It's time to talk serious issues miss Jasmine, not one of your evening dreams or sudden absent mindedness. So, where were we? Ah! Yes, do you know Jasmine what had happened yesterday in school? Clearly no. As you were absent! So, let me tell you that one of the fairies of our academy was found dead in a store room, where he might have gone to pick more copies, and most importantly, do you know what evidence was found at that spot? A witch's amulet! Can you believe it? The most feared thing is now becoming real! That is why we had held a meeting last night in Arcane to discuss out a plan to find the culprit!" Arcane was actually, their secret hide-out in the school. It was a medium sized hall, with a few light bulbs hanging on the ceiling and it was actually an old laboratory for conducting experiments which was now abandoned, and almost no one came there unless for some cleaning! This news definitely got Jasmine and she screamed in terror as well as in anger, "Oh my god!! How dare they! How could they kill one of our school mates? This means that, Violetta didn't say it just for the sake of saying! She meant it! And now we are in danger. Guys, I also need to tell you something, I was asleep---"

"SHUT UP" said Terence pointing out to some neighbours peeping at their group with curiosity. Now only one place was left for them to talk, inside the peach tree! Yes, it was a special magically grown tree-hide out by all five of them, inside which was a quiet, calm and peaceful area to talk. There was a small stream flowing by, and Lavenders were flourishing all around! The scent of lavender present there, itself was enough to calm them down. The moment they headed towards the tree, Brandon's phone rang, "Yes? Oh, mom. Yes, I will be back, ok bye. Guys I need to leave, Mom is alone at home as my little sister Scarlett has gone for an excursion trip, you know already." "It's ok Brandon, we were also not very willing to listen to what Jasmine wants to speak!" said Alice with an annoyed expression, she took Rose by her arm and left the park in a few wide steps. However, Rose didn't really protest but she literally felt bad for her best friend, at the same time disappointed. Soon after, the boys also left and Jasmine was returning too, with a broken face, and misery was written across her face, "that's not fair", was all she thought and headed to her house. Well, that really wasn't quite fair, they could have at least listened her out. Okay, that night, none of them could sleep peacefully as they never had such an issue hanging over their heads!

But this was enough to set ablaze Jasmine's heart and soul! She felt completely abandoned and thus decided that instead of mourning her state she must do something to show them that she wasn't such a mess! "Okay Jasmine, let's do this! You can do it! I will go on my own after this scroll and I am sure the one who wrote it was Violetta. So, all I need to do is to find her and directly confront her! Yes! I have no choice. No one trusts me and I can't just sit by and watch these evil witches kill us fairies! What would I need, yes, some fairy lights, a map to Witchtopia, a compass, some spell books and my wand as well as some fairy dust!" she quickly gathered the important things and packed them all in a small bag, then she put on a dark red robe and black boots and tied her dark brown hair into a high pony. After that, she quietly slid open the window of her bedroom and off she went into the night sky for an unknown search, assuring herself that she had not just committed a huge blunder. It was twelve minutes past one, when she was flying through the clouds which were already getting wild. It seemed like a thunderstorm was about to hit! "Hmm, if I continue on this route right now, I might get into trouble" she thought. "It's better if I take some rest on that acorn tree, I really need to know where I am. Have I left Magic Meadow behind? Or not? Maybe, I am somewhere around the border. Oh God! It's so foggy and cloudy tonight!" So, she stopped in her tracks and settled on a tree branch where a cluster of golden acorns was hanging. She plucked one of those and it tasted really nutty, while she relaxed, she didn't forget what a threat she was going to face all alone. Honestly, she didn't know any of the defence magic so basically, she was unarmed, except for her wand made of acacia wood and was ten inches long! Well, that could protect her but not for a long time against those evil witches. In a few moments, tiny droplets started raining down on the ground and she waited patiently for the right time.

Back in Magic Meadow, Terence, could not sleep because of her little sister's snoring! So, he got up and went out in his herb garden for some fresh air. "What a pity! Now I can't even sleep peacefully!" he murmured under his breath as if uttering a curse. The herb garden in his house was placed such that it directly faced Jasmine's house and he could easily see what she was up to! So, he thought and tried to peep in her window but for his surprise he found that the light was on! "What is she doing at two? Is she mad? I should better go and check before she causes any more trouble to any one of us now!" he growled just as his pale golden wings appeared and he flew towards her window. Lights on, things were thrown here and there, some peculiar objects were resting on her study table while her wardrobe was open and it seemed like someone had been rummaging through it! Obviously, it was Jasmine. The moment he realized this, he blasted into her room, "what the hell?! what was she planning to do and where is she now? No, this will make things worse, you idiot girl! She was talking about sharing some important news but we didn't let her speak. Damn it! How can I be such a fool? It must have been something important! Not that she concerns me but this whole situation can cause havoc as it's a very real danger to us, all. Fairies can be in a serious problem. I need to go after her, wherever she has gone! There must be some clue!" and he started searching her room madly when he found a torn piece of paper lying on the table. It looked like a map. "This might be it; this might be where she had planned to go, she might have forgotten this torn piece here. I need to take this with me, it can help to locate her whereabouts!" So, he took the map and some pouches of fairy dust, slid open the window cautiously and off he went to look after a girl he disliked the most! Or maybe just to dodge a life-threatening danger and save his people? Whatever it was, it was getting intense now.

VI

The storm had been really as beautiful as much as frightening it was. Finally, when the rain stopped and the glowing thunder bolts had taken a halt, Jasmine decided to resume her journey. She picked up her little cloth bag which she had hung on one of the branches under the tree shade, and flew into the sky! "Huh, finally I can fly. It was so boring to sit idly on that tree, although the acorns were quite tasty. So, now I need to check my compass to see if I am going in the right direction. Hmm, where's the map? Oh, I got it! Uhh, yes! It is north from this route and my compass is also pointing that I am heading towards the right direction! Thank the fairy god mother!" she wiped her forehead with relief and was headed to the north when she realized where she was as the clouds started fading away and she could easily see the ground beneath. "Oh my god" was all that she spoke softly as she recognized that place from one of her textbooks of history, it was 'The Dark Woods'. It was an extremely dangerous place, especially for fairies! Why? Because tales had been told about these woods that many dark powers and spirits wandered in here and waited for a prey to feed on! Not only to satisfy their hunger but also to suck out all the magical power out of their preys, so that they could become more powerful! It was nearly three at midnight, when the evil energies were at their peak! "It's ok Jasmine, it's ok! No need to get scared, ok? Yes. I am a fairy and that is why I need not be scared. Just don't look down. Ya right, Heads up and eyes on map. That's it!" As she was flying above the dark woods, she suddenly heard a howl.... of a wolf! 'Awooo' and she picked up pace, as she flew swiftly above the silver glowing clouds in the starry night sky. But there was something that caught her eye, the moon. It was as big as a planet and seemed to glow a little reddish and dark green! "Oh no, just be quick be quick!" she told herself, suddenly her vision faded and she accidentally fell on a hill top! Before she could realize what just happened, she saw something sparkling inside the petals of the fern plants growing there. "What's this? Are you mad? Just go! No, what if it's something useful? I must go and see." So, she moved forward with caution and her wand ready at her side, when she saw what 'that' actually was. It was a small crystal box in which some old paper was neatly kept. As she cautiously opened it she saw, that there was a painting of some sort of runes on it! There were pictures of four runes on that paper, painted with extra care & precision. What was it? Was it some sort of clue? But to what? That exactly was troubling her mind when she heard another howl. She immediately, put the box in her bag and in a second, her gorgeous and little wet, peach and silver coloured wings took her up in the cool air! That was a close call. But it was like, falling from sky, finally nearing the land and then getting stuck again on a big bushy tree! Yes, the moment she took off, she hit a giant cedar tree and fell down with a thud! "What the---" she growled in pain. Before she could stand up she realized where she had actually fallen! It was a bewitched muddy puddle! Which was now just pulling her body in and in deep. Her wand was also broken and surprisingly her spells were becoming useless! She started screaming, which was a real foolish step. But you know girls, right? Anyways, when she was almost sucked in till her neck, a shadow appeared at her back side which she saw in her front, because of the moonlight. The shadow was tall and lean, and to her shock it was quietly observing her, despite her screams, with a gesture of folded arms on his chest. With some difficulties, she managed to turn her head around, almost thinking of seeing a dementor maybe, but what she saw, was, what made her scream a little louder, but in rage! Haha! It was, Terence! He was standing their quietly, looking at his nails! Then he looked at her and grinned. "Oh, I see you are done screaming? So let's not waste our time anymore right?" "Are you insane?!! Help me out! Now!" just as she said this the puddle had sucked her mouth in and it was exactly when Terence glanced at her, in a real serious look, and with one swish of his finger, she was thrown out of that bewitched shit! 'BANG!' she flew out of the puddle and hit the ground with her back. "What the heck! Couldn't you catch me?" This time he really did look amused as he said, "Oh, I would take that into consideration the next time you fall" and he grinned again. But then the wide smile on his face was again replaced by an unreadable expression. "Jasmine it was really foolish of you to go out here all alone, I can't believe you can be such an idiot!" he frowned while she helped herself to stand up. "Oh really? Did you even listen me out? No. So, I thought that I----" "Thought what? Just stop giving excuses and come with me, then you can tell us what you know, and we will work it out together", he said with a half-hearted smile. As she had no choice left, she did as she was told, and again, failed miserably in gathering some much-needed optimism. "I don't know why but my magic powers are not working, Terence. I don't think I can even fly." "Wow, so now I need to carry a girl as heavy as yourself, right?" he asked, with a tired face. "Oh yeah you certainly have to", she uttered the words, as if she was about to beat him up any moment now, for insulting her! Well, she really was not even one percent obese, who knows why he said this? Just to tease her? Never mind egoistic and stupid guys, just about half an hour had passed when Terence got really tired of carrying Jasmine's weight on his right hand, as he held her by her arm just below him. So, they stopped near a cave in the forest, after he checked if that area was safe, with his self-made Magical Radar which could easily detect negative frequencies. The two of them quietly settled in the cave and he also put on some fire for warmth in that cold, shivering night! "I guess the dark magic in that area was so powerful that it sucked your powers too, though for a short time." he said while his eyes were on the dancing flames. It seemed as if, he himself was burning from within, because of his fairy friends out there who were now suffering by getting either killed or going missing! But then, a gentle hand was laid on his shoulder which emitted pure warmth and concern of a true friend, it was Jasmine's hand, "It's ok Terrance, we will work it out, all right?" the moment she said this, she started shivering when a cold breeze touched her cheeks. Was it just a cold breeze? Or something else? Being a fairy, born with natural gifts, she could sense danger in the air too. "Hey, I think someone is there! Hush! Be quiet" said Terence as he was an expert in this particular *'psychic magic & sensing abilities'*, of course. He quickly covered her with his body and took out his wand, when a shadow stepped in front of them! It was a witch! Not 'some witch' though, it was Percy! Violetta's bestie! "Percy? what are you--" Jasmine was about to move forward when Terence stopped her quickly, holding her wrist. Before he could start any negotiations, Percy, with a swift movement pf her hand, pulled out a dagger and was trying to strike him and helpless, he had to cast a self-defence spell, *'protecto'* as the witch flew backwards instantly. Still as a statue, she lay on a nearby rock! "Damn it! Is she okay?" He thought and strode towards her body lying motionless. Nope, she was dead, she was not breathing! DAMN IT! What had they done? This was not something Violetta was going to spare them for! "Let's be out of here quickly after burying her body properly with respect, alright?" Terence murmured softly to Jasmine, with an expression of suppressed guilt. So, they did, and flew off after placing a red velvet rose on her buried body. It took almost an hour and a half for them to get back to Magic Meadow when he dropped Jasmine in front of her house and so that he could get at least a few hours of peaceful slumber, he slept on a folding cot in his herb garden as the darkness engulfed them. Tomorrow was going to be A BIG DAY, as both of them had decided that they needed to tell this whole scenario and explain the situation to their best friends, because they had to save them. They had to save Fairyland, at all possible costs.

VII

It was a heavy day as the sunlight peeked through the silver clouds, ready to snow. "Wake up, darling. It's morning already!" Jasmine's mother chimed in, as she entered her room, with a broom in her hands. Obviously, she definitely had an intention of sweeping away...invisible dirt! Hahaha. But of course, she was merciful enough, today as she let Jasmine skip school. Little did she know, when she thought her daughter was tired; that a huge black stormy cloud was hanging on her head, constantly. "Uhh, ya mom, morning." She murmured quietly, thinking deeply about last night. As she pondered, the realization hit hard! Yes, today was the day when she would actually have to reveal her discovery to her only friends! But, thankfully this time, she wasn't alone - Terence would be her support system. "Mom, I am going to take a bath and then will be off to the park, okay? Sorry, no time for breakfast today, though." She said as she made her way to her cozy little bathroom. Just as she shut the door behind her, she unlocked her smartphone and texted in their chat group - *"Hey, could y'all please skip school today? Some real important things to discuss! Please meet me at CRYSTAL COVEN @ 8:30, sharp."* A few times her phone buzzed, probably with replies from others, but she couldn't look, for at the moment, all she wanted to do was take a long, warm shower and forget the stress of the day even for a few minutes!

"Wow! So, what do you think you wanted to say when you decided to cancel our schools today?" Alice jumped in, in pure frustration as you know how she was quite a short-tempered tom boy. "Alice, it's okay. At least let Jasmine speak up or put up her point here, right?" Rose calmed her all the way down as she still secretly, was dying to know what in the world her bestie was up to! "Okay. Now, no more ramblings. Jasmine, speak up. I advise you to start from yesterday night if you wish", Terence gestured her to go ahead as she was shaking a little. Finally, she gathered the courage to speak, not for her own sake, but for the whole fairyland! " Guys, see there is a mild---no huge problem coming for us. Actually, I had found a letter in my bedroom a few days earlier, at night. It was delivered by a red-eyed owl! At first, I couldn't make it but then I realized it was a threat written in blood, by Violetta! It warned that she has been planning something devastative for us fairies...all this time, while she was being silent! " Immediately, the air was charged with tension, all the false anger got diffused, as after a long gap of silence, Brandon spoke up with a frown on his forehead, " WHAT THE ACTUAL--- " "Shut up! Jasmine, are you crazy? You should have told us earlier, no matter what! God, how could you keep something so big from us?", screamed Rose as she cut off Brandon and struggled with her own little bestie-betrayal. "Oh, c'mon man! You thinking of yourself right now? How petty, Rose," Brandon shot back. "Enough! " This evidently, came from none else but Jasmine, as she fought against the looks of perplexity on her friends' faces, boldly. "What? There's nothing we can do by fighting! See, I have not completed the story yet. I went out last night, on my way to Witchtopia. Okay, no comments, only listening first. All right?" "Hmm, go on J..." The group spoke in unison as Terence tried genuinely to count the number of leaves on the peach tree! Lol, emotions are too heavy to handle sometimes, aren't they? "So, what basically happened was, that we accidentally.... umm, striked & killed Percy, Violetta's BFF, while Terrance was trying to just protect me by disarming her as she pulled out a dagger! Guess, he put a little more force than required or maybe lost focus while casting the spell. So uhh I, I mean 'we' decided to---" "What the hell!?" All three shouted together as panic crept over their terrified faces. At the end, Alice had the courage enough to speak up, "okay, guys, calm down there's nobody's fault in this, okay? Jasmine & Terence had no such intention to harm Percy. However, she definitely had beautiful plans for them!" "You are right Alice; the whole question now arises here. Did Violetta actually go to the extent of killing them?! If yes, that is probably right, then we are in for a real danger here." Rose explained as all the words and facts sank into their skin and left fearful marks! "All right we got to do something here as we all know the damage can happen in real, any time now." Brandon panicked, when he added, "I have got a plan, it's risky and all, sure. But it's all we have got. I suppose we have to break the fairy laws and school regulations once again." Everyone was deathly still, listening to him quietly, when Rose sighed, "that's it, done with the suspense. Spill it out Brandon, what do you have in mind?" There was a certain hope reflecting in his eyes at this, "Alright, Terence & Jasmine, you two are the most familiar with this case, so I guess you two are the best and only options, this time. I, I guess both of you will have to *go to Witchtopia, in disguise as a witch & warlock; get admission in Wiggenweld Academy and dig out the main plan. For that I can create a portal after a few days of practice, and then, you are on your own wits, skills and magic."* There was a frozen silence in the park. Even Terence didn't speak except the very noticeable twitch in his jaw. Finally, the host broke the silence, "Soo, are you all set? Because once you dig out their plan of attack, you will have to send me a message through a ring I will ask Alice, to give you both. And... then you come back.... & maybe afterwards, we could fight back, all prepared", he finished on a hesitant note that made chills go up Jasmine's spine. Well, she certainly didn't have any idea that, this was how the day was going to take a toll on herself and her friends. Anyways, this was all they had got, truly spoken by Brandon. Just as the sun started to set, the Mystery Gang realized, it was... Show Time.

VIII

The night was chilly and eerily quiet when Jasmine, tossed from side to side on her comfy princess size bed. Only one thought raced in her mind at a speed of thousand electricity bolts, "what could possibly go wrong when we get our admissions in disguise? I hope nothing. If we get trapped, we need to have a backup plan, as well." Finally, hours passed by and it was clearly about time for the sun to rise as one could see the bright tint of red coating the dark skies! As she stole a look from her window, a new bud of hope and faith germinated in her heart, for the morning always represented a new victorious beginning! It had been three full days since they decided their secret undercover mission. Everyone was secretly hoping that Brandon wouldn't fail them...obviously, he was the best Alchemy student! Where Jasmine got ready for the day, with a little bit of makeup, a flowy knee length, pale blue frock and lots of courage.... Terence didn't even bother to take a damn bath! He paced back and forth, in his herb garden, mind spinning with certain possibilities and only one goddamn thing gathering most of his attention - "why in the hell, do I need to go with her!? I can *easily* take this whole mission out, on my own!" He thought to himself when his little sister... ehmm, much accurate to say- the famous little trouble; Lily, came running and jumping up and down as she screamed picnic. Duhh, wow. What a timing Lily, really. Anyways it took real labour to dodge her questioning looks and a threat to get back at her brother with some silly prank, after which he managed to somehow, escape to Crystal Coven. Everyone was already there standing in a circle, while in the centre was Brandon, with his eyes closed, trying to form a portal, nothing to worry about, as their activities were being blocked by a huge illusionary hedge created by Jasmine. Another matter of fact, today was actually their lucky day as everyone in the society was busy in the preparations of Christmas, thus they were all, out of their respective houses at the time. "Be quick, Brandon! Anyone can come anytime now", exclaimed Rose. Just as he was busy focusing on his powers and mixing a certain quantity of gooey liquids...a thought struck Jasmine's mind as an alarm. "Wait, wait! What about our costumes before we get admission? I guess we **need** to dress up, really!" "Oh, please! Relax J. I took care of that already. I put those outfits in your secret handbags. After all, beauty & guise spells have been my all-time favourite, you know that already.... here take these and put them on", Rose winked & chimed in with her usual easy charm. It literally took five minutes for Terence to get changed after he clutched his outfit of a warlock in his palms and went behind a tree. Coming out almost instantly, and properly dressed in the disguise costume. Whereas for Jasmine, she took an equal amount of time, only gazing at hers, ever so fondly! Girls, again. Her costume was a dark forest green gown, with an overcoat- the colour of night. A pair of black boots and few other witchy accessories. When they both got dressed up, it was time for morphing their faces...a little. Obviously when the portal was ready, Brandon did this privilege by providing two small cups of some strange looking, purple brew and after a few more minutes they were all set with their communication gemstone rings on their fingers. These were specially made by Alice as she was an expert with crystals and gems. The noon had started to fade away and dusk was stepping in when they realized it was time to go. God! As in, literally. The portal was a shimmery sea green hue and emitted bright sparks! "It's time, my friends. Go on, give hell to those wicked witches. I believe in you... **we** believe in both of you!" Brandon spoke up as he fought back nervousness from lacing his words. Just as the main society gate creaked open with a shrill sound; in they went, without a glance back... heading for something too unknown, too dangerous. And at the same time, something too important to now, run away from. For the sake of their land and those innocent lives...

"Wow. I mean, umm, astonishing! Isn't it?" Jasmine whispered in her partner's ears slowly as they landed in the middle of a scary looking yet eerily gorgeous forest. There were tall pine trees surrounding the edges and fading away in the distance as the air was covered with thick silver fog. Yeah, way too eerie. "C'mon, let's not waste any time here wondering about the history of this forest! We got a huge mission, remember Jasmine?" Terence scolded her, as he strode forward with long and wide strides, nearly leaving Jasmine behind on the trail. "Hey, do not teach me alright? I am after all the best student in class, remember?" Ahh, there it was, the scowl on his face! But of course, it was the sourest spot in his heart, that he was always the second! LOL. The moon was full and high up in the sky as both the fairies...in disguise, made their way out by ducking under bush after bush. A little time flew by when, finally they passed on to the only clearing in their visions! "Phew, finally the creeps are over!" Jasmine murmured to herself. A little more walking and they eventually saw a huge wooden, semi-circle shaped board on the top of two bamboo pillars. It read, *'**The Olive Village.**'* "Hmm, 'The Olive Village', this seems like the right place to spend one night and make a few allies, doesn't it?" Terence glanced at Jasmine, who was currently busy adoring the huge landscapes of olive trees. "Yes, right. We might as well, dig out some important information about Wiggenweld Academy!" After a little planning and discussion, they memorized their role plays as two siblings and pushed the old rusty gate open, with a slight creak. It was 3:00 AM at night, so they assumed everyone would be probably fast asleep. When they were about to knock on one little door, another opened up behind them. "Hey! Who are you? And what are you doing here at midnight?!" A frail old witch came out who was walking on the support of a bamboo stick. With extra politeness, Jasmine spoke first, "sorry to disturb you ma'am. But we were actually passing by the Dark Woods and our car stopped abruptly. When we examined, it came out to be an engine failure! Eventually we decided to walk down the forest and came here in search for shelter for one night only. Uhh, yes, we actually are siblings who got admission in Wiggenweld Academy for Witches & Warlocks", she explained calmly while Terence nodded in agreement. "Oh! I am so sorry dearies! I thought it was some sort of thief, ha-ha. No worries, dear, we have one spare cottage in our small village, the boy can stay the night, there." Alarm striked their minds, but they fought it on their faces as hard as possible. "What the hell!? We ought to stay together. We have to discuss so many plans for tomorrow and contact our friends too!" they both thought in unison. "See, ma'am, we are both close siblings by relation; I am Jessica and this boy here, is my brother, Ted, and so we would be quite comfortable to stay together in one cottage. I wouldn't like to interrupt anyone else's sleep tonight, as well." Jasmine tried to negotiate politely after cooking up two suitable names for themselves, whereas Terence simply nodded at this one, too. God knew why there was a slight frown on his entire face as he struggled to agree with Jasmine's words!? Maybe, he was tired. Or maybe, there was something too hidden in the background? Anyways, after a little convincing they got their cottage for the night stay and contacted their friends, Alice, Rose & Brandon immediately. When all was settled, they finally went to sleep on two tiny beds. However, both of them were well aware that none of them was actually going to sleep. Why? Obviously, they were preparing.... preparing for tomorrow; because tomorrow they were going to give a damn good shot to their acting skills as well as, put to test their very own, FAITH....

IX

The morning came like a heavy challenge, as Jasmine opened her eyes slowly, taking in the reality weighing heavily on her thin shoulders. She got up and brushed her teeth when a realization struck her. Terence was nowhere to be seen in the small cottage! "Damn it, where are you now Mr. Weirdo?" A frustrated sigh escaped her lips. Hastily, she put on her black overcoat as the morning breeze was quite chilly, when she made her way out of the cottage, to the olive fields. There was a tall and broad man's shadow leaning behind one tree, as she made her way up to him. "Ha, what a nice view right? You could have even gone straight to Wiggenweld for some fresh air, right Terence?" Her voice dripped with anger and sarcasm. Obviously, how could he leave her behind in that cottage in an unknown territory like that? What if something had happened?! All these thoughts frustrated her even more. "You know, I really wish I didn't bring you with me, it would have been much easier." He complained with a bored look on his face. Just as Jasmine was about to explode like a grenade, a soft voice called them from behind. It was the old, kind lady from last night's encounter. She wished them good morning and offered a hearty breakfast, including - candied olives with sugar syrup, that topped luscious thick vanilla cream on those pineapple pies, a crystal glass full of mango juice for both and crisp, golden brown banana bread slices. "WOW. Simply, wow. This is incredible!!" Jasmine 'whisper-shouted' in delight. Terence too, was so dumbfounded, that he couldn't even utter a word at the sight in front of him, it was literally Heaven! The old witch smiled gently and asked them to feast upon the food, as much as they wanted. And so, they did. After their bellies were full enough, Terence stood up gracefully and hugged the old lady with a sweet smile full of warmth. "Thank you, for your favour ma'am, we couldn't have found a better place to stay last night. I really wish you happiness and prosperity in life ahead, because you are one of those people who really deserve it." He spoke quietly, as if lost in deep thought. In return the witch squeezed the life out of him and kissed his forehead. "Oh, my boy! I do wish the same for you two! Go on now, get yourselves to your destination - Wiggenweld Academy. But do not forget to pay back a few visits every now and then, is that a promise?" "YES!" Both of the fairies laughed as they hugged their new friend though somewhere, they knew they wouldn't meet the sweet old witch again. As they bid their sincere goodbyes to the villagers, they whispered to each other, "it's time, buck up partner."

"So, here we are. What do you say, Terence?" Jasmine proudly pointed out to the **huge** castle like school right in front of them...or should I say, in front of the edge of a cliff they were currently standing on? Really, it was a tremendous sight to hold! There were high, dark green mountains surrounding the Wiggenweld Academy, from all directions. Far in the left was a huge sparkling waterfall, running down the deeper, disappearing valleys! So basically, they were dumbstruck. Oh! Definitely, it wasn't like that thing called comparison, The Cloud Castle Academy wasn't any less. Instead, if ever held, there would be horn locking competition between the two of them! No idea, which one would eventually win, but right now this wasn't on their minds. In fact, right now they were in their most analysing and calculative versions! Specially, Terence as he took out his frequency detecting radar, to check if they were being watched or something. Fortunately, they weren't, as he told this to Jasmine. "Alright J, we got to cook up a new story, one that explains how we as two best friends and students, lost our brooms and wands while we were riding down the hill towards the Academy. Presenting ourselves as blood related, isn't a very great idea here; it could rouse many questions and we won't be able to answer all of them. And we say, we were robbed by some nasty goblins, okay? I found this extra bit of information in a book, back in Magic Meadow that goblins have a liking to these grounds." "Uh-huh. So, when do we give the witches...I mean Violetta, a little surprise?" She asked with determination and a hint of mischief. A smirk covered his mouth as he winked in her direction and that very moment, both of them slid down the slope of the cliff... ready for another interesting and witchy encounter!

"Woah, slow down man. At this speed, we would probably end up in the creek down there, our heads buried in mud!" Shouted Jasmine, in utter shock, as they were nearing the foot of the cliff. "Oh? I didn't know you were a scaredy-cat?" Terence smirked as he reached out with a hand to hold hers. After a few more minutes of suffering against the rugged, rough and rocky slope...they finally halted at the bank of the rippling creek. "Well, that was a pleasant ride. Now let's make up for this one by giving a literal hell to dearest Violetta", Terence spoke with irritation, as he picked himself up and quickly strode ahead, confident as ever. Jasmine followed behind him until she matched his pace. Together they walked for about an hour or two when lastly, a huge tower came into view that had walls as high as the sky itself! They took out their fake identity cards and the fake admission confirmation letter, one for which all the credit went to Mr. Terence Williams, of course. "Shove it in the empty slot, right there." He whispered as he pointed towards her identity card, all the while avoiding and sometimes smiling politely at the curious and intense looks of those witches & warlocks buzzing in and out of the tower gate, which was supposedly the school's main entrance. "Okay, here we go", said Jasmine just as she and Terence, both swiped their cards and the small light bulb turned green, granting them access to enter. "Oh look, who's that duo? Maybe new comers. And by the way, nice looking guy, that one" Ah! There came the first comment as a group of three young witches passed by glancing mainly at Terence. Now, for the first time there was a scowl on Jasmine's face, while he tried to hide a smirk. What was going on? Whatever it was, none had any idea... as their eyes were solely fixed on the school inside as they walked down the aisle of nightmares and prayed to the Fairy Godmother that they would at least receive a *normal* welcome, even if not very warm...

X

The air was thick with worrisome thoughts racing in both of their minds as they treaded forward inside the main school area. There were huge staircases lined with pure silver, at the far ends of the vast expanse of marble floor, they were currently standing on. A large number of students, both witches and warlocks, were running up and down the steps and some were casually gathered in a group, chatting about the weather! "Oh, I don't know how we would ever fit among them!" Jasmine panicked a little while Terence was having his gaze fixated on something..."hey, what are you looking at?" she asked as they halted suddenly and Terence motioned her to now part the ways with him. "What? So suddenly? Why?" "Because, it's time. I already see some students giving us weird glances, besides, we ought to introduce ourselves as good friends, but separately. Now, let's head to the principal's office using separate paths, so that we don't seem that close. Clear?" "Yup, boss." Then they actually moved in opposite directions, where Jasmine kept glancing back nervously, he didn't even look back, for once. "Oh, my goodness, okay relax Jasmine, you can do it, yes without any hesitation. Imagine as if you were a real witch, yeah, here I come, Wiggenweld." After a long search for the office, Jasmine finally arrived at one with a name plate on it - '*Mrs. Rehanna, Principal*'. Just as she was about to push open the door slowly, it flew open on its own! "Ah, Miss Jessica, please come. We were expecting you." Immediately her guards were up as she focused on the 'we' part, and her gaze landed on the third person in the chair, waiting for her - Terence Williams. "What the literal heck!? How did he get here so fast!" She thought, but schooled her features effortlessly. "Hi Jessica, I hope you didn't get lost? Well, I have told our story to the principal and now you may show your admission letter to her, please. Ma'am, as I informed you, she is my childhood friend and we have come here to attend Wiggenweld Academy and make our fellow witches and warlocks proud." Terence spoke with his usual air of confidence and ambition. Just as Jasmine got seated and showed her letter, the principal spoke up, "hmm, interesting. Really interesting. I have seldom seen such ambitious and talented young students in my school. As a matter of fact, you two are most welcome in my academy for we certainly do need young talents!" At this, she signed their admission letters, without looking twice and gave them their dorm room keys and assigned an escort to each of them. "Thank you, Mrs. Rehanna, we will not let you down", both of them spoke in unison and exchanged a secret glance of victory, while they got escorted to their respective hostels and once again, parted ways. However, this time there would not be any chance of getting lost, this time the aim was pretty clear.

The corridors were dimly lit with a strange hue of sea green, as Jasmine crossed them one after the other. Her footsteps echoed across the stone floor, and long shadows were cast on the huge stone walls as well, on her either side. A long silence passed when she finally dared to speak, "umm, if you don't mind, can you tell me where are we exactly?" The escort was a short stout woman, who seemed to be extremely serious and scary by the way she glanced back at her, with a smirk playing across her thin lips. "Of course, dear. We are crossing the forbidden towers", she said with a long look on her face as they now treaded up a giant worn out staircase. "You shall get your school uniform by tomorrow morning, till then stick to your dorm room, you can go to the canteen for snacks but remember to return back quickly. For, a new comer like you would possibly get eaten up by the seniors here, if got noticed", she said softly, and for the first time Jasmine felt a feeling of warmth coming out from that strange woman. She listened quietly and nodded at times, while the lady kept giving her basic instructions and told her about the rules. "Ah, here we are, your dorm room. This is the girls' hostel, so feel free here." Jasmine looked up and saw a beautiful teakwood door in front of her that was covered with strange little climbers. "Thank you so much, ma'am. I will receive my uniform tomorrow at time and shall remember your given instructions." She said politely. After the lady left with a formal good luck, she stepped in and closed the door behind her back. "Phew! What a day!", just as Jasmine was checking out her little comfy bed and a small iron windowsill, a sweet voice sounded behind her back. Jasmine immediately jumped and turned around, only to meet her new roommate - a young witch, who was currently in her bath robes! "Oops, sorry I will just go out and---" "no it's fine. After all you aren't a boy! Hahaha....well, I am Rix. And you are?" "Oh, umm, my name is Jessica." After cooking up her new alias name within a few seconds... Jasmine replied cheerfully because she really was in a good mood, if this witch was going to be her roommate! She definitely needed a girlfriend to hang out with, and not to forget she might be her first ally! After they chatted a little about each other's backgrounds.... obviously, that had made Jasmine cook up another story; they decided to explore the canteen as Jasmine came to know...fortunately, Rix was a new comer too! That made them even. While Rix was busy getting dressed in a dressing room in the corner, Jasmine decided she would wear her gorgeous silky yellow frock with black stockings and a pair of sandals. Just as Rix was done, she went in to get ready and pinned her hair in a high ponytail and a few barbie clips here and there....and finally they were all set to fill their bellies and for some meet & greet!

"Wow...this is magnificent!" Rix whispered in Jasmine's ears, as they stood in front of the large canteen of Wiggenweld. "True, but I doubt we will get something as lame and loved, as cheese burgers, in here." Jasmine replied back, as they went in, a small goblin was placed at the door while he scrutinized their faces. "Ignore them. They are just naturally suspicious creatures" Rix spoke in a low voice. When they finally spotted an empty table, they literally dashed...just as Jasmine was getting seated, she turned her head sharply as she spotted a very familiar face in the crowd.... yes, it was Terence sitting with a few guys, nearly three tables apart. His gaze was also locked on hers as he silently inquired, if anything went wrong. She simply shook her head as an answer, for now. Anyways, luck was on their side, as they got their order quickly - two full cheese burgers! Both Rix and Jasmine squealed in excitement as they dove in. They had also ordered two glasses of strawberry shake as they gulped it down as fast as possible! Yeah, those poor girls were really hungry. "Ha, now I feel recharged, what about you Jess?" Rix smiled, as her friend answered, "I Am Alive, now." This was followed by a hearty laughter booming out from both of their lungs...as others glanced at them curiously. "Hey! Shush...I am going to just dump the paper plates in the bin, okay? Then we will head back to our dorm." Jasmine said, as she stood up gracefully with her hands filled, she walked towards the bin, when suddenly the canteen door flew open with a loud 'thud' and before she could react a tall figure bumped in her back! "WHAT THE HELL!?" Oh My God, she knew this voice... a little too nicely. She turned around with frozen hands and saw Violetta standing right there, with her hands on her hips, blurting something filthy to her three cheer leaders! Before Violetta could return her gaze to the obstacle in her path, Jasmine moved as swiftly as a lightning bolt and disappeared from her sight. She stood in a corner while everyone got deathly still, waiting for Violetta's approval to carry on, maybe. However, Violetta immediately picked up her chicken salad, and stormed out. Rix took that exact moment to run up to Jessica, her almost gone friend. "Oh my gosh! Are you okay Jessica?" she panicked, and all Jasmine did was nod. For Violetta was as shrewd as she thought earlier, but this time, she left a little trail for her as her last words to her minions, were still ringing in Jasmine's head - *"All set now, just gonna meet that piece of shit tonight! Then I would show those fairies their real place."* "Alright V, go ahead, because tonight I am going to follow you" Jasmine mused while she conveyed an urgent meeting to Terence through her eyes, using the power of telepathy as he watched her intently. Tonight was going to be a spooky fun....

The pale-yellow moon was slowly rising up in the sky, when Jasmine quietly crept out of her hostel, and headed for a little out house that was actually a spot for storing basic school supplies and a few water filters. Yeah, that was where she and Terence had decided to meet right at seven. Because it was safe this way, as the hostel gates would be closed everyday by six thirty sharp! So... basically, she had climbed the wrought iron gates with her too known sleuthing skills that came in handy. Obviously, she had been careful enough to keep a watch on her surroundings and her back. Now, there she was standing behind a pile of spare and unused copies in a corner of the outhouse, when she heard footsteps moving in her direction. Although she had an idea it would be Terence, she still was on high alert, with her wand at ready! And... the door flew open. "Hey, what's up?" Terence said casually as if it was a birthday party. "Oh god, it's you only! Alright, now first come and sit here," she pulled a chair out of the corner and he looked at it with utter distaste. "Oh really? Do you expect a fancy couch in here?" "Of course not. Now, don't waste my time and spill the secret. What did you gather as a clue, from Violetta?" He said with a shrug as got himself seated on the little chair. "See, I heard a line she was possibly passing on to her minions. She said she would be going out tonight to meet *someone* who would probably help her in her plan to attack Fairyland! Who do you think it could be huh?" she asked with a curious look. Terence simply seemed thoughtful for a while, before he finally spoke up. "I guess, we need to find out. For that, we will have to follow her, we got no time as she might be leaving now or might have already left! For once, listen to me J, let me do this chasing and I promise I will come back to give you all the information, okay?" To his surprise she laughed comically for a while then said, "I guess you still have not succeeded in knowing me Mr. Williams! I AM GOING, TOO." The firmness in her tone literally caught him off guard and he had to agree, obviously.

Just as the clock struck nine at night, both the fairies tip toed to the central tower gate. This was followed after Jasmine had bravely sneaked into the senior witches' dorm area and Violetta's room had a lock on its door, which was enough to confirm that her suspicions were true! But as they treaded slowly towards the gate, she had her mind on a different plane as she felt guilty about not telling a very big part of this whole story, she hadn't told him about the secret box with a strange painting of four runes, that she had hid in her bag when coming to Witchtopia. She herself didn't have the answer to why did she keep it? It might have been nothing. But there was a peculiar gut feeling, telling her to do so. Now this was still a big mystery! Who was the sender of this strange box that she collected when she was stuck in the woods, that night? Why did it find her, out of everyone else? What were the runes trying to tell her? Why did she always have a feeling of getting an answer when she gazed at the painting?! Like, she was very close to something, but then it always slipped away! Well, there were a few questions running a marathon in her mind when, Terence whispered, "Jasmine, I have bewitched the gate for three hours, exactly. I couldn't do more than that, so that's all the time we have got tonight. Let's be quick and stay alert." He instructed as she was nodding, thinking how they would manage to snoop out some real information in such a short time period! They didn't even know where and how to start! Well, maybe she didn't know! Anyhow, when they stepped outside the school building, a rush of chilly wind swept past them, as they were searching for a trail with wide-open, hawk eyes, Terence immediately nudged her elbow, and before Jasmine could ask further, he dragged her quickly behind a square junction. "There, I think, that's the car she's riding in right now! C'mon, it's time we give a try to our newly polished brooms, ready?" "Ya, let's---wait, what? Brooms!? You never told I had to bring mine! Besides, I don't know how to fly one Terence, this is ridiculous! Why not use our wings simply?" Jasmine shouted in a low voice, as he rolled his hazel-coloured eyes, with a real force. "Do you think I didn't think about *that?* Of course we can't use our wings, stupid! The witches' radars here, will immediately detect fairy dust and our true identities!" Wow, this was quite a celebration tonight. Their plan was about to fail even before it had started! "Now, what?!" Jasmine whispered hastily, as he came to a conclusion that they had no choice other than getting her seated at the back of his own broom. Just as she was about to contemplate and argue... a little, he summoned his dark brown broom and mounted it at once. "No time to waste or we will miss the trail, Jasmine. Now, c'mon get yourself comfortable for a bumpy ride." Yeah, it was actually going to be bumpy as she was already having a panic attack while mounting the broom! Lol. No wonder why she had a hard time when she first learned to fly with her tiny wings! "Just.... DON'T scream", he warned and in the flash of a second, they were up in the sky. The clouds roared with lightning sparks and the trail was clearly visible, downside; as they rode across the sky in search for a secret landing....

XII

It had been an hour or so since they flew off the academy grounds. As Terence was busy directing his broom, there was a clear perplexity appearing on his smooth face. "What's the matter? Is the trail clear?" Jasmine asked worriedly for she almost **never** had seen so much stress on her friend's 'all prepared face.' "Yeah, all good. It's just that there is too much fog up here and...and I think we are treading towards dangerous grounds, Jasmine" he spoke softly, as if waiting for a horrified reaction or something. Jasmine was clearly neither horrified nor surprised, because she somewhere knew this was leading to unknown dangers! And wouldn't it be a miserable failure if she now, let her fears take over? No, she wasn't going to let that happen! Instead, only one thought made her fears retreat back in the shadows - she and Terence **had** to save Fairyland, at all costs, even if the cost was their own lives. So, in a nutshell, they couldn't back out now, they had to be brave, brave enough to resist their weaknesses! "Don't worry for me, Terence. I promise, I won't back out now, in fact, I would never! So, it doesn't matter how dangerous it is where we are heading to, we got a whole bunch of fairies to save! I believe in myself and I believe in you. I know we will make it." "Yes, we will." That was all he said as he appeared to be really touched by Jasmine's faith in him and herself as well. And for the rest of the ride, they both went silent as the broom led them hovering above, from one alley to another, following the silver car. It was strange the way Violetta's car was taking twists and turns, every now and then. Finally, after another thirty minutes of chasing, the sleek car came to a halt, in front of another dimly lit alley, which barely had any houses! "That's it, this is where she was headed to, J. Now we have to land, be still and don't utter a word, please", he ordered as the broom started descending, slowly. The wind was howling madly, for some unknown reason maybe, as Jasmine struggled to stay still so she clutched the back of Terence's shirt tightly. Just as they landed in complete silence, Violetta got out of the car, wearing a weird long black robe and gothic jewellery. In a matter of a few steps, she was inside a very strange looking hut, as she shut the door behind her back! "Okay, now we got to spy, right?" Jasmine enquired, and her partner nodded slightly. Slowly they crept towards the window... only to witness a sight that blew their minds off.

"Hmmm..." A very unfamiliar voice, hummed in the silence. Not to mention the sound was really a quirky one, it almost sounded like, that of some malicious beast! Then came the shrill and high-pitched voice of the witch, they had followed, "are you even listening, you idiot? You have to send your armies now! It's time and I am losing my patience, as well. Afterall, DO NOT forget I paid you a generous amount, for this little mission! Once those Fairies are wiped off the face of the lands, we will get to rule together! As I promised, I will bring your community in light and you will have your own kingdom. Is that clear, Imp?" "Interesting, alright, witch. Consider it done. Just remember you don't get to boss an Imp around...and, by the way, did you bring the key to the North Pole so that we could first wipe out that shit? As you said, that will be our first move. For the filthy fairies are expecting their Santa and his elves on Christmas eve! It would devastate them to know that all those pieces of shit are dead. Ahahaha! I would so very much enjoy that scene!" "Yeah, on that one, I don't disagree with you, Imp. Anyways, I have to leave now so be off tomorrow morning with your army for I will deliver the four keys to you, by the time you reach North Pole." As she uttered those last words, she stormed out of the little shabby house and stepped into her car. "Oh my god! Terence, your broom! C'mon we got to return too! Quick." Jasmine spoke hastily, in hushed tones and both of them were practically up in the sky in the next few moments as they chased Violetta's car to get back to the Academy. They were finally nearing the school grounds, as Jasmine spoke up, "I can't believe this! They are going to destroy North Pole!! Then they will attack our home land, those evil and cruel Imps! I never knew they still existed! We **have** to return to Fairyland, now!" "Shush! Stay calm, J. I know we have to leave but we can't do so without a proper closure, otherwise we will be caught and kept as prisoners here, in Witchtopia... forever! First, we need to find out what those four keys are that provide entry to the North Pole. I am not going to sleep tonight, I have loads to research on and find out! We are here now, Jasmine. Stay as much in the shadows and on the side lines as possible, and play your part. Good night." He whispered as they landed in front of the main gate and immediately Terence made a dash for his boys' hostel, without another word. After a minute of shock and panic, Jasmine did the same and reached her dorm room, constantly staying in the dark, as she was told. Quietly she turned the door knob and shut it noiselessly. Fortunately, Rix had not woken up as she slept soundly in her bed. Just as Jasmine changed into her PJs, she was alarmed by a sudden thought or maybe, a realization hitting her hard! Violetta's words were now, bouncing in her head like a ball! *'**Four keys...**'* "What the actual hell!? How could I not think of this earlier?" Jasmine was practically heaving with excitement! Because she now understood, what were those four runes on the painting, most probably representing! Yes, those were the keys to North Pole!! And that painting was a literal clue to identify what they looked like! "Oh, my Fairy god mother! What am I supposed to do now? One thing is for sure, I won't get to sleep tonight."

XIII

It was three at midnight, when in the boys' hostel, Terence was wide awake as he kept searching for any information regarding North Pole and the history of Imps, their biggest weaknesses and much more! For the first time, he closed the books that he had stolen from the library, scattered on his study desk, rather disheartened. For he couldn't find anything that relevant, except he had actually discovered, that Imps were scared of fire or any natural source of light! Maybe, that's why they never came out in sunlight and always remained in the shadows! Well, if this was the case, then how would they manage to attack Fairyland? That's it! It clearly meant that they were planning to attack at the time of nightfall! "Hmm, at least this discovery is something. I need to urgently contact Jasmine and give her all the input." He rose up from his desk and because fortunately he had got a single room, there was no one to worry for. Just before he was about to open the door of his dorm room, a weird looking pigeon came flying and sat on his window sill, with a letter in its beak! He jumped into action and carefully extracted the letter after petting the pigeon on its tiny grey head, as the bird quickly flew away. "Who has sent this? I need to see at once", he thought before he tore off the envelope and immediately recognized the handwriting! It was Jasmine! Without wasting another second, he read the letter out, - ***"Terence, it's urgent, we have to meet. See, I have something to tell you, now. Please don't be mad at me because I had actually, all this time, kept something from you...I think it's time you know about it. Because I guess, I know what the four keys to the north pole are!"*** ...."What the heck, J!?" Before he could throw away the letter in frustration, for being kept in the dark, he managed to listen to his rational mind and read further, ***"But we can't meet at this time, so I have decided we will discuss the matter in the canteen tomorrow. Rix isn't going to be a problem, as she woke up in the middle of night and told me she won't attend classes tomorrow because she felt sick. So, I am free to be alone, got it? Need to sleep now, see you soon."*** Woah, tomorrow was a real mystery to Terence, no doubt in that. But he decided that to do any more work, he also needed some sleep. So, he slept, not that soundly but sleep did come eventually... shielding both of them from their nagging fears and giving enough strength to face the wicked coming their way.

The morning came quite swiftly, as if daring Jasmine to get up and face the challenging day, ahead. And of course, she was not the one to back out! She hopped out of her bed, without disturbing her new friend, Rix. For she suspected she really had started caring for her. And why shouldn't she? Yeah, she was a witch too, but she was not Violetta or even anywhere near her! And obviously, to think that all witches were bad was something she could never do, it was truly being a person who believed in stereotypes! And she, certainly, was not one of them. So, she silently stepped into the bathroom, and brushed her teeth, in a slow and lazy motion. Then she took a nice and warm bubble bath in their little bath tub after which she got dressed in her newly received uniform. Well, one would have to say that the uniform was actually, good. There was a checkered skirt of knee length and was dyed in baby pink colour, where the top part was a plain white shirt with crisp collars and little gemstone buttons. Then came, the overcoat dyed in dark forest green, that almost appeared black from afar, and lastly a pair of white socks with dark green boots, same colour of the overcoat. When she was ready in her uniform, she piled up her silky brown hair in a high ponytail with the natural bangs she had at the front and stepped into her leather boots. Somehow, getting dressed in Wiggenweld's uniform, made her feel more courageous! "I don't know if we will succeed or not, but what I do know, is that we will try our best to stop that wicked witch! We will find the four runes or keys and save both, the North Pole and our Fairyland" she told herself in the mirror while she gazed at her own reflection. "Time to move, Jasmine." And she opened the door of her dorm, ever so softly, as she headed straight for the canteen, along with the painting of runes, in her pocket...

It hadn't been long since Jasmine arrived at the bustling food counter, ordered a few grilled cheese sandwiches and sat down on an empty table; that Terence finally came into view. "Hey, please sit. We got loads to discuss and a whole less time to act" she said with an air of urgency but didn't miss the look of betrayal on her partner's face, as he sat down quietly in the chair opposite to hers. "Go on, spill it" he said casually, or at least pretended to be that way. Thus, she started to actually spill it, because she started from the night in the dark woods, when she had first noticed the painting, hidden between a few plants. Almost half an hour passed as she continued to tell him everything, and finally stopped at the conclusion that they had to find those runes, immediately! "You might be right, there is a slight possibility that those runes are probably hidden in here, in Wiggenweld only", Terence concluded. "Because this is where Violetta lives, plus, whosoever sent that painting to you, was clearly indicating that the runes or the four keys are somewhere in her reach or probably she already has them" he continued, "which means we have to get those before she does! And we clearly have an advantage with that painting, you got, in case she doesn't know what they look like." Now, Jasmine was intrigued, "what makes you think that?' She asked, "well, when she was talking about the keys to that Imp, I detected a firm note of uncertainty in her voice. She might be on the hunt right now, J" he sat up, alarmed. Jasmine too sat up straighter, as she spoke in a low voice, "where to, first?" "I suppose, it's her dark arts class right now, she might be somewhere near the back towers!" Terence hastily, ate up his sandwich and so did Jasmine, before both of them, turned towards the exit door and marched out. It was a long way to the back towers, and they were extra cautious as these towers were forbidden for the juniors. So, obviously they wore a black robe covering their whole body, and a floppy hat that made them appear as some care taker staff. After crossing a number of staircases, they neared a big classroom, with a board on it - *'**Dark Arts**,'* "hey, we better hurry as our own flying class is soon going to begin!" Jasmine murmured, when they reached the classroom, and peeked in without being noticed; their suspicions were right, as Violetta was not there! "She couldn't have gone far on foot, c'mon! Let's see where she is headed" Terence ordered as he strode forward, towards the end of the corridor. "Where are you going? That's a dead end! We need to take the stairs" Jasmine shouted as she followed behind. "Seriously Jasmine? Do you think Violetta would actually take the stairs to wherever the runes are kept? Anyone could notice her; she must have taken a hidden passageway!" This hit her hard as what he said was actually logical. Together they started searching for any clue in the stone walls, when her hand swept over a darker stone. She carefully examined it and pushed a little harder, before she could say anything, the stone shifted and so did the others around it! "Woah, stay back, J. I think you found it" Terence praised her, as they saw the stones getting apart, opening up a hidden passage, full of cobwebs and green flames, lit in the corners! Without waiting for a new obstacle, they dashed in, putting their lives at stake, to save the lives of those they loved....

XIV

The cave like passage, was a real scary deal for those who were faint of heart! The green flames in the corners, licking at the walls furiously, were casting long eerie shadows as both Terence and Jasmine, treaded further, cautiously and equally prepared. The farther they went, the more did the secret passage become eerily dangerous..."I really hope there are no ghosts in here", Jasmine pleaded to the Fairy God Mother, hoping she would listen or maybe come to their rescue. "I don't think there's anything to be scared of, because after all, if this path would have been dangerous, Violetta wouldn't have taken it on such a short notice." Terence assured her, confidently. "Oh, and why do you think *this* was the path she took? What if we are on a wrong trail?" He simply sighed, and rolled those gorgeous eyes of his, of course; but then he explained as for, why had he come to this conclusion, "don't you see Jasmine? First, this was probably the only hidden passage near her classroom, at that time; second, she definitely went down this way because the evidence is clearly, visible....as it's imprinted on the stone floor, see, right there!" He pointed out to the lightly soiled imprints of someone's sleek boots in front of them! Now, it was practically crystal clear to Jasmine, why he was so confident and how he was leading the way out of some unknown hidden passage in an unknown territory! Finally, as she gave up on overthinking, Jasmine found something shiny in a particular corner, Terence was walking at a fast pace so she decided to stop him, but another voice in her head told her that maybe she should just pick it up as she thought she had seen it somewhere, and move on without a word. Maybe she did so, because somewhere she knew that he wouldn't pay attention to some piece of jewellery! Or maybe, he would...she just felt safe to say nothing at the moment. As he told her that they were probably nearing the end, and there was a slight ray of light coming in, Jasmine got a close look at the little garnet ear ring she had picked up. She peered at it curiously, when recognition hit her! "It is that gothic piece of jewellery, Violetta had worn the day before, when she went to meet that Imp!" she thought, and was about to disclose her bigger evidence confirming that they were on the right path, when Terence suddenly pulled her behind a strange looking rock. "Hush, I heard footsteps approaching! Be quiet" he said, just as someone appeared in their line of sight! It was none else, but Violetta! Except...she wasn't alone, as they had suspected. There were two wicked looking Imps with her! "Here, now go and be extremely slow and quiet! I know where those runes are but I just cannot identify them! Oh Gosh! This is frustrating. Go, tell your master to move with his troops and DO NOT inform anything about what happened here, clear? Now grab your gold and get lost!" Violetta ordered with a bit of irritation. "Terence, this is our chance, we can follow her to where the runes are being kept, hidden!" Jasmine said hopefully, where he seemed absolutely grave, "J, we have to be *very* careful now, give me that painting" he demanded, as she fished it out of her left pocket, handed it over and also disclosed her little garnet secret. "Good, now follow me". Exactly at that moment, after the Imps had left, Violetta turned around on her heels and went deeper into the dark shadows. But what she didn't know was, that two of her *beloved* fairy friends, did the same, following after her in the darkness, stealthily and filled with powerful intention...

After walking in the shadows for a while, they finally saw Violetta reach out for a knob in the wall. She turned it down and slid inside but just before the sliding wall could close behind her leaving the two fairies baffled with an uncertainty...they made a run for the chamber inside, and fortunately got in without a scratch! Wow, maybe Fairy God Mother *was* listening to their prayers! "Oh my god! This is beautiful!" Jasmine exclaimed in utter awe but before she could speak another word, a large hand closed on her mouth, and grabbed her by the elbow! "It's me stupid! Terence. Stop babbling around like a kid and see our target is right in front of us!" She lifted her gaze to see that Violetta was figuring out the runes, as she had her back to them; all those three people stood in front of a huge heap of various types of runes...it was like a heap of gold! They glistened as if they were polished! Each one had a unique symbol on it. It seemed like a long time, after Violetta broke the ice. "I have to do something, find some clue, some hint...urgently! I have to deliver the keys to that Imp!" Just as she stormed towards the entrance of the chamber, she spoke a password, **"Ariana"** and the wall opened and then, closed behind her back with a loud noise, as both Terence and Jasmine kept pin drop silence. "Okay, here we go, Jasmine, c'mon... let's dig into the heap of these runes and find the keys!" After a long searching they eventually identified three same looking runes just as in the painting. Now, only one was left, and anytime Violetta could come back! Jasmine looked at the painting for the umpteenth time, and memorized the fourth rune... a beautiful pale parrot green colour and a unique gold *sigil* on its surface. As her eyes roamed everywhere, they stopped at one spot, "there! I think that's the one!" She cried in victory and marched towards the shining little beauty. And guess what, that rune, indeed was the one, they were looking for! In a haste, they once more, matched those runes with the painting for confirmation, and quickly dashed out of the chamber after speaking the exact same password, 'Ariana.'

While they were walking back towards the corridor, Jasmine spoke up, "I wonder who Ariana is. Why would Violetta keep her name as a password?" "Because, she - Ariana, is Violetta's late *first* mother, I found this out when I was researching, you know". Terence answered after a deep thought. "Do you remember, how she reacted back in Cloud Castle, when that ring of hers was broken? She said it belonged to her mother", he explained further. "Oh yes, now I get it. She must be very attached to her first mother, obviously" Jasmine concluded, too. "Now, matter of importance, we have to immediately get to North Pole. For that we have to make a risky run for it, for we aren't left with any other options! We have to chance it, Jasmine. As you know, we already have missed our flying class today without any given reason, so slight suspicions can arise, and Violetta can anytime return to that chamber and find out that someone was there, because you probably dropped your bracelet inside..." he pointed to her empty wrist, with a finger. Before she could scream in horror, he pulled her aside and gave a warning glare that made her realize that they were now at the passage entrance. They simply couldn't afford being caught, here. "I am sorry. Anyways, what do we do now?" She asked earnestly, as they stepped outside without making a single noise. They soon realized it was dusk by now, "now, we contact our saviours, our friends. C'mon, let's find a safe hide out, somewhere near!" Luckily, after a few steps only they saw an empty classroom, which was probably the one of dark arts and they entered inside quickly! In the blink of an eye, they started rubbing their rings furiously, hoping for an immediate response, which didn't come. They had started to discuss another escape plan when Jasmine's ring started glowing! Immediately, they held it in their palms together, and a shimmery screen appeared. Then the worried faces of their friends got clearer as one of them shouted, "what happened guys?! We are scared as hell! Do you need to escape?" This came from Brandon, before Terence responded quickly, "Yeah, you got it right bro. How can we escape right now? I mean, it's possible right?" "DO NOT worry, I am going to create a portal right away! Hang tight, don't lose connection!" Just as a faint shimmery ball of light started forming in the air, in front of their eyes, the classroom door flew open! "Hmm, we have guests here, don't we?" Violetta spoke with a sneer on her face, as she took out her wand, and in a flash, their morphed faces were... *gone*! Their wings emerged, glittering and glorious.... but their Fate? It seemed like their fate would have seriously betrayed them, if not for their friends! Because the second she began to cast another spell, most probably the one for knocking someone out nice & clean... the enormous portal, that Brandon was creating, grew into its full form and sucked them inside in a few seconds! And they were plunged into a darkness leading to a light; full of hopes and chances, once again!

XV

"**I** don't believe this! How in the hell, we got caught!?" Jasmine shouted in agitation as they fell deeper into the shimmering and swirling portal. "You know, if for a second you thank the heavens that we were saved by our friends, instead of complaining...it would be really nice!" Terence retorted. After a few full seconds, Jasmine realized that her partner was probably right...what would have happened, if they had been held as prisoners in Wiggenweld by, Violetta? Or more precisely, what would have happened to their loved ones, if they had been dead! Wow, some real nice thoughts, Jasmine had her brain stuffed with, when suddenly, their fall ended as they landed on soft mud! Before Terence could make a remark, Jasmine started hopping happily, because they were now in Fairyland, exactly in front of the peach tree in Crystal Coven! "Finally! Home sweet home! I love you my Fairyland--" "If you really do, then be ready to make another trip to the North Pole" Terence said, casually, while he brushed off some dust from his pants. Just as they stood up and took in their familiar surroundings, a group of three people charged straight for them! Obviously, the saviours. "OH MY GOD! Jasmine, Terence! Are you two alright?" Rose screamed in panic & relief as she hugged her best friend and

Terence, both. At that exact moment, the warmth coming from her best friend's words, made Jasmine's heart ache, for she had left someone behind, whom she really considered a friend, Rix. "Rix, how could I ever explain to you? Would you ever understand? I hope that no one harms you, for the scene I caused in Wiggenweld!" she spoke softly, in her mind. After explaining their extremely dangerous situation back at Wiggenweld, both Jasmine and Terence looked tired, but none of them confessed. "Hey, let's go to Magic Food Mania, for some delicious meals and a little light talk...what say?" Alice asked softly, and all the four of them agreed almost immediately. After freshening up and getting dressed in decent clothes and also meeting their family after a long time and dodging tons of questions, Jasmine and Terence along with their friends rode down to MFM, in Brandon's car. It was a long ride, but provided enough time to think over their recent adventures, as they both silently gazed out of the window, with their minds still lost in a maze....

After, grabbing some hot cocoa and bubble-gum cream filled buns, the mystery gang, sat for long hours in the cafeteria of MFM, and chatted about their next moves. When twilight set in, Brandon finally gave the last statement, "so, it's decided. Myself, Alice and Rose are coming with you two to the North Pole. We have equal urge to protect our nation and our happiness just as much as you have. The point is, when do we leave? According to what you explained, those Imps are on their way but missing the keys, and we have them! Now we just need to get going" he concluded, quietly. "Right, bro. I suggest we do not delay and may as well, leave early tomorrow morning!" Terence said, as he stood up and gathered all the plates and some leftovers, which he dumped in the nearest bin. Just as everyone stepped out of the food mania, a chilly breeze attacked them, wildly. "I know it's silly, but I think I already feel something wicked in the air", Rose sighed and her shoulders slumped, sadly. It was probably a sight, too heavy to bear for Brandon as he came closer and wrapped an arm around her, comforting her and assuring, as well; that together, they will fight...they won't let the darkness take over the light! The night came in a few hours, when everyone was back in their houses, in their warm beds, but none was actually asleep. "I bet, that Violetta is trailing us currently", Jasmine mused as she lay in her cream coloured, fluffy bed, staring out the half open window. "I don't understand one thing though, who is helping me all this time? Who gave me the biggest clue to stop the evil plans of Violetta- the runes' painting? I may not be aware of that person now, but I am aware that he or she is our well-wisher! At a time like this, we need one. Good night to myself, for tomorrow it will be a bad day for the Imps......" and she fell asleep, ready to awaken for a dawn that promised victory!

"Is everyone ready?" Brandon asked for the last time, as the friends stood, all prepared, in front of the icy looking portal. He waved his hands as the portal expanded after everyone nodded with an approval, "all right then, here we come, North Pole" and they stepped in before, all of them were plunged into it, as quick as in the blink of an eye! In a few seconds, they found themselves shivering with the icy cold wind, blowing at an abnormally high, speed rate! As they lifted up from the snow-covered ground, they saw a **HUGE** gate made of frozen diamond and delicious looking lilac jelly! The jelly was flowing in weird shapes that formed specific sockets of different sizes and appearance. It seemed like it was meant to be filled with some objects in order to enter North Pole! "It looks like the Imps haven't reached the gate yet! C'mon let's hand those runes to Santa after we open the gate! Hurry!" Terence announced, as he snatched the keys from Jasmine's hands and placed them carefully in the sockets resembling each one's size and shape. Almost instantly, the gate started to move apart, permitting them to witness a vision, they could never have imagined! There were thousands of elves rushing from one place to another with different coloured gift boxes of all sizes and shapes...in their gloved hands! In the centre was a huge Mansion, covered with all the Christmas decors, even the fairies couldn't create or buy! Just as they started moving towards it, a heavy and fluffy laughter stopped them in their tracks! "Ho-ho-ho! My fairy friends came 'ere for a visit, eh?" A large plump hand covered their shoulders, as all of them jumped together! Behind them stood, The Santa! Immediately Rose, Jasmine and this time even, Alice were drooling over the cutest sight they had ever seen in their lives! Not to mention, Terence and Brandon were both, trying to hide the adoration in their eyes, constantly! "Ehmm, Santa. We are here to actually warn of an attack by those evil Imps. They can be here any moment now. Please take these four runes or the keys to North Pole and close the gate forever...so that no one could access it without your permission", Terence explained the situation, softly and handed over the runes. For a second, he thought that he saw a knowing smile on Santa's lips. When one full minute passed, it was confirmed that he wasn't imagining, for the Santa was indeed, smiling! "Ah! My sweet peas, you need not to worry! For those Imps have been misguided by are naughty little Christmas elves!" He winked at them. They got dressed up as them, and successfully guided them to a path leading to their own territory! Ho-ho-ho.." this certainly made the fairies more relaxed, and they finally smiled too. But before anyone could say another word, Santa handed them five different boxes wrapped in sparkling gift papers! "Merry Christmas, young fellas!" He said happily as he walked towards the mansion...that was his home probably. "Listen here! We ought to return to Fairyland as quickly as possible; we need to know what's happening there right now and keep our guards up constantly." Alice remarked, and after a little more planning, everyone agreed.

The moment, they stepped out of the portal that opened in the park, Brandon fell to the ground with a thud! Rose rushed to his side instantly just as everyone else did, thankfully, he wasn't unconscious but he definitely had put all of his magical energy for making those portals! That's why he had collapsed! "You urgently need rest, Brandon" Terence declared as he told everyone to get back to their homes as he would stay with Brandon for the night. A few hours later, Jasmine and Rose were taking a stroll in the park when an idea struck Rose's mind, "hey, J. I guess we should open our gifts and see what did Santa give us? They might be special weapons or something to fight against Violetta!" "Yes, you are right, let's do one thing, we all should meet at Brandon's for he is there with Terence right now. And we will take our gifts with us", she said as she texted the same in their group. In an hour, there was a proper meeting set up at Brandon's cozy house, "okay, let's do it." Brandon said out loud, as he tore open his box, only to find a small vial of some pale green liquid! "Wow! Santa knew that I will be tired as hell and that's why he gave this healing potion to recover quickly!" He shouted delightfully as his friends urged him to drink it instantly, and so he did before he felt ten times more powerful! "C'mon, go on with tearing those pretty little wrappers off", he said enthusiastically. Next was

Terence as fished out a strange device which probably startled him before there was a huge grin on his face...."what is it, Terence?" Alice asked curiously. "It's a literal, power sucker!! We got to be very careful with this one, it should not get in anyone else's hands. Wait, let's give it a try! Rose, keep that wand of yours here, now." Rose was horrified, but she obeyed, obviously because being a fairy meant you could have lots of wands for just a few silver stars! When Terence switched on the device and kept it near the wand, the little wood stick, literally broke in three pieces!! "Awesome, we can also utilize this power as double now!" He chimed in with barely contained excitement. Alice's patience broke too as she tore off her gift and found a box of colourful, mind-reading crystals! And then came Rose's turn, "wow! I have got a disguise mirror! I can change my form by looking into this with an intention!" Now all eyes were set on Jasmine's box, that was practically the smallest. "Uhh okay, here we go", she said softly, as she unwrapped it and found a small pouch containing few very peculiar looking golden seeds. After a moment, she recognized what it was! "These are the fire growing seeds! Also, they are unlimited," she said and picked one up when instantly another one replaced it! "But wait, why fire?" Jasmine asked aloud. Quickly Terence rose up with a smile, telling them his little discovery, "because Imps are scared of any natural resource of light...which also means they are attacking us at night. And... this also means one more thing, why did Santa give us these 'now?' Because Violetta is probably aware by now of those misguided Imps, and I am pretty certain that they have already been redirected & are finally headed towards our Fairyland. Let's be prepared because tonight, my friends, we are being attacked....

XVI

The snow was falling constantly on the streets of Magic Meadow, as slowly and slowly, the night was coming to greet them, with a dark gift in her hands. By this time, just as Violetta had decided to come all prepared, the fairy friends did the same. They had told all the fairy ministries and their Fairy Queen about the massive attack coming tonight! There were royal guards positioned at the boundaries of Fairyland, where the Queen had herself come down to the main City Square. Their queen, Azure had never been a coward, even after the death of their generous king, Arnold. And right now, she was fully armed and ready for a face-to-face combat! The Cloud Castle had also been informed about every detail, regarding the upcoming war. The whole school was prepared, as they had volunteered to be a part of the Fairy Army, and so did the Mystery Gang! It was eight at night, when the five friends were guarding the river line border along with other guards. "It seems like they are really approaching, see that green tint at the edge of the sky!" Just as Rose uttered these lines, a terrifying cry broke out, in the silence, along with emerging figures, of blood thirsty Imps!! "Jasmine, quick, throw the fire growing seeds, now!" Terence commanded her just as she took some out and threw them as far as possible.... immediately, there was a roaring fire licking at the skies, as a barrier between them and the Imps. "What's that?? Look out!" The Imps cried in utter horror, as they started retreating one after the other, nearly jumping over each other! Clearly, these dark and foul creatures couldn't bear the impact of light! Well, good for them, then. But just as they were running back for their lives, a huge cloud burst occurred and a bolt of turquoise lightning fell directly on those filthy Imps! "Oh, I always knew you pests were good for nothing! I will kill you myself!" A maniac laughter sounded across the skies, when a thin and utterly wicked figure came out of the shadows - it was Violetta! She was riding on her broom just a little high in the sky as she killed every single Imp, left. "Is she mad?! She is killing her own army?!" The guards shouted in genuine shock. At that very moment something came up in the minds of Terence and Jasmine as they bravely stepped forward and shouted together, "Violetta! Come and fight us! You need to know that good always wins, and the wicked always loses. We challenge you!" A malicious and disgusted expression took hold of her features as she jumped to the ground, furiously. "You are the cause of all this drama, Jasmine! You broke my mother's ring! You insulted me, ME!? You tried to overpower ME! I will not forgive you; I will kill you!!" Suddenly an urge to end this all for good, came up and Jasmine pushed Terence back towards the royal guards as she ran forward without looking back! "No! Jasmine! You Idiot!" Terence tried to call her back, but she didn't even halt or turn. Apparently, Jasmine had something in mind, he didn't understand. "V, look we don't need to---" "Don't call me that! You are not my well-wisher; you are my ENEMY! DO NOT pretend!" Violetta shrieked, but Jasmine continued, "I know Violetta, why you are *what*, you are. I know that a gang of wicked and ill-willed fairies had killed your real mother out of envy a long time back, I know that's why you hate us soo much!" An extremely shocked face was confronting Jasmine, now. Violetta's mouth fell open as she slumped to the ground, "you don't know anything, NO!!!" It felt like an even strong wave of bravery washed over Jasmine as she too sat down and touched her shoulder gently, "I know everything, for I always wanted to know more about you, know more about why do you hurt others.... I obviously never admitted this to anyone but, I was waiting for this exact moment, Violetta. I personally dug up your past and the reason behind your deep hatred for the fairies, with a lot of hidden efforts that not even my friends knew of. I was waiting to see how much you loved your true mother. Because if you really loved her, you would never be the same as her murderers. You would never harm us fairies for the exact same reason, those fairies killed your mother for! Hatred and pleasure. There would be no difference left between you and her killers then, your mother would never want her daughter to be one of those demons, who didn't have the right to be called fairies!" By now, there were tears streaming down Violetta's face, as she struggled to say something, anything. "Sshh, you don't have to explain, now, come with me and together all of us fairies and witches shall celebrate Christmas!" As Jasmine picked her up, Violetta looked into her eyes deeply, with her jade ones, and said, "You are right, J. I will always love my mother, *always*."

It was Christmas eve, and all the witches and fairies had gathered, in a huge ball room to celebrate, as Jasmine, Terence, Rose, Brandon & Alice stood in a corner, and watched the dancing couples and friends with delight! After what had happened the day before, this very day called for a

GREAT celebration of happiness and joy! Even Violetta had brought a dance partner, her brother - Victor, who was a powerful warlock. The sight was a treat to everyone's eyes as large crystal chandeliers hung above, from the ceiling and moon dust was sprinkled in the air! Although *that* caused some people to actually sneeze at intervals! Lol! "Hey, Rose. Would you care for a dance?" Brandon extended his hand (which was shaking a little), and Rose immediately blushed. Everyone else had suddenly developed an intense liking to those minor decor items in the hall as they tried not to acknowledged the interaction between two of their friends! Hahaha! A little awkwardly, Rose took his hand and he swept her off her feet as they danced in the centre of the Ball room! A soft pat startled Jasmine, and she turned around to see, her friend, Rix! She was grinning from ear to ear when she hugged Jasmine tightly. "Now, I don't need explanations! Let's dance...besides, I am fascinated by your Fairyland, it's such a pretty place!!" Later both the beautiful friends, twirled on the marble floor in the ball room with pure grace and joy, while Terence and Alice did the same... also, not to mention, Alice gave a look to everyone, that said she would very much prefer a basketball competition over the whole cheesy waltz! Typical, as the tomboy she was. And Terence, well, he had his gaze helplessly locked on her, as he watched Jasmine laugh and dance so happily! Just then, a loud & bubbly laughter boomed outside, up in the skies before the happy crowd rushed outside! All the friends were delighted to see the magical show in the clouds above, and to witness another shower, this time not just of snow balls, but of thousands of colourful presents and tasty candies as well! People grabbed their treats and gifts in a sweet frenzy, while the five fairy friends gazed up at the big sleigh with reindeers, flying across the night sky, cutting through the thick clouds... whispering to each other, with a smile reflecting relief and happiness, "*A Merry Christmas.*"

THE END

THANK YOU FOR READING!

Hey my lovely readers! I want to say thank you that you gave your precious time to read my first novel ever! I would never forget this, for I love you all as much as I hope you love the adventures of Terence, Jasmine, Alice, Brandon & Rose! I will definitely publish many more series of WINGS! I already have a lot of ideas invading my mind, ha-ha! Also, I would love to hear your feedback! Please email me here - **smritibakshi2002@gmail.com** if you want to leave one. I wish you all love & light filling up your lives, and tons of creativity! There is a very special quote, that I simply adore, here it is, "***If you want your children to be intelligent; read them fairytales*** " - ***Albert Einstein.***

We will meet with another magical story, very soon!

Love you all.... **XOXO**